Where Do I Fit In?

by June Noble

illustrated by
Yuri Salzman

Holt, Rinehart and Winston / *New York*

Text copyright © 1981 by June Noble
Illustrations copyright © 1981 by Yuri Salzman
All rights reserved, including the right to reproduce
this book or portions thereof in any form.
Published simultaneously in Canada by Holt, Rinehart
and Winston of Canada, Limited.
Printed in the United States of America
10 9 8 7 6 5 4 3 2 1

Library of Congress Cataloging in Publication Data

Noble, June.   Where do I fit in?

Summary: His mother and stepfather are
expecting a baby and John is not quite sure how
he fits in to the family.
    [1. Family life—Fiction. 2. Babies—Fiction]
I. Salzman, Yuri. II. Title.
PZ7.N669Wh   [E]   79-1073   ISBN 0-03-046181-2

For my stepson,
John Alden Noble

"Why are we going to the zoo?" asked John.

"Because it's a nice warm day," said John's mother.

"Because the mama elephant just had a baby," said Charlie, John's stepfather.

John said, "I just went to the zoo with Dad."

"When?" asked John's mother.

"Last weekend," said John. "We already saw the baby elephant."

"Don't you want to see him again?" asked John's stepfather.

"No," said John. "It's too cold."

"Then what do you want to do?" asked John's mother. Her voice got higher, and John knew she was upset.

"Stay here." John put his head against his mother's stomach.

He knew his mother and stepfather were going to have a baby because they told him. It wasn't a secret, but John did not tell anyone, not even his best friends.

John's stepfather, Charlie, pretended to box with him. "Hey, champ, I have a better idea. If you don't want to go to the zoo, let's go by Fred and Jane's. Mom and I will go to the zoo and you can stay with them."

John liked Fred and Jane, who were Charlie's parents. Mom called them his new grandparents. They lived near a lake and Fred took John fishing. Jane made sugar cookies for John.

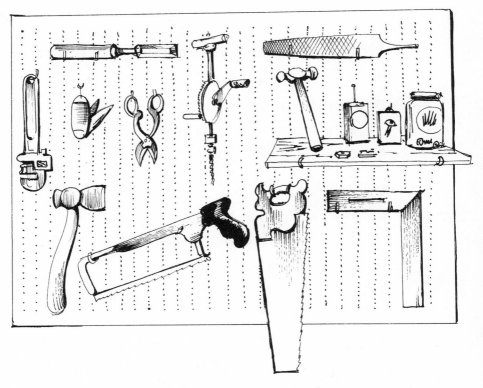

"Sure," said John. So his mom and Charlie dropped him off on their way to the zoo.

John found Fred in his workshop. He was putting hinges on a small box. "What's that?" asked John.

"Climb up on that stool so you can help me," said Fred.

"It looks like a box," said John.

"That's right. A bait box."

"Why are you making a bait box, Fred?"

"For my grandson," said Fred.

"Oh," said John. He climbed down from the stool. He wondered how Fred knew the baby was going to be a grandson instead of a granddaughter. "I guess I'll go in the house." John had a lump in his stomach and couldn't tell if it was a sadness lump or a hunger lump.

Fred dropped his screwdriver on the work bench. "Hey, wait a minute, John. You can help me put on the handle first."

"I don't know how," said John.

"I'll show you. In a few more years you will do this in school."

John didn't want to, but he climbed back up on the stool and held the handle in place so Fred could screw it down.

"Thanks, John. Now I'm going to make it waterproof. Then, when my grandson goes fishing and gets it wet, it won't hurt the box."

"That's good." John got down and ran in the house before Fred could stop him.

Jane was not in the kitchen. There were no cookies baking in the oven. She was sitting in the living room knitting something red. "Well, John! What a surprise! Are your mother and Charlie here?"

"They went to the zoo," said John.

"Without you?" Jane seemed surprised.

"I went with my dad last week. They have a baby elephant."

"Fancy that," said Jane. "Just like our family. A new baby." She put down the knitting and ball of yarn. "Did you see Fred?"

John nodded. He didn't want to talk about Fred and the bait box, so he pretended he didn't care. He stuck out his chin. "Mom says I can stay with Nana and Pop next summer. I'm *their* grandson."

Jane smiled, "Well, that's sure to make them happy."

John's chin went out further. "And my Gram and Gramp are getting me a caboose and boxcar for my trains. They're my dad's parents, Gram and Gramp. I'm *their* grandson too."

Jane had a worried look on her face. "Is something wrong?"

John mumbled, "Fred said he's making the bait box for the baby."

"The baby! What would a baby do with a bait box?"

John said, "He said it's for his grandson."

Jane laughed. "But that's you, honey. You're his grandson." She held up the knitting. "Here's a hat I'm making for *my* grandson. That's you."

The lump in John's stomach started to smooth out. He said, "Mom and Charlie call you my grandparents, but I wasn't sure."

"Then I guess you better start calling me Grandma Jane."

"What about Fred?" asked John.

Fred walked into the living room. He was wiping his hands on a kerosene rag. "What do you mean, what about Fred?"

"We're talking about your name," said Jane, "and what John and the baby should call you."

"The baby isn't even born yet," said Fred. "I'm more interested in what my grandson calls me."

John looked at Grandma Jane and Grandpa Fred. "Do you know what?"

"What?" they asked together.

"I have three grandpas and three grandmas."

"That's pretty nice," said Grandma Jane.

Grandpa Fred said, "Well, it's better than a poke in the eye."

Grandma Jane clapped her hands in a way that meant business. "Tell you what. I'm tired of knitting. I know you're tired of working in the shop, Grandpa. And I know you're tired of hanging around, John."

"What's your idea?" asked Grandpa Fred.

Grandma Jane said, "I, for one, would like to see the new baby at the zoo. I haven't been to the zoo in fifteen years."

"Neither have I," said Grandpa Fred. "I used to love to go to the lion house and see the lions in their cages."

"They don't have cages," said John. "They walk around free."

Grandpa Fred was really surprised. "You mean the lions aren't behind bars?"

John said, "They walk around rocks. There's a big ditch between them and us."

Grandma Jane said, "You mean the elephant and baby are not in cages either?"

John said, "Nope. If they kept them in cages they couldn't have babies. They would be too sad."

Grandpa Fred said, "John, that's the fifth new thing you told me this month. Makes having a grandson worthwhile."

John felt more important than he had for a long time. "Do you want me to take you around the zoo and show you everything?"

Grandma Jane didn't waste a minute. She ran for her coat.

Suddenly she stopped in her tracks. "Do you know what?" she said. "We just might see your mom and Charlie at the zoo."

"That's okay,"said John."I'll tell them I changed my mind." And he really had. He had changed his mind from worried to happy. "Maybe we could all have lunch together," he said.

Grandpa Fred said, "Sounds good to me.
I guess you're the leader, John. That sure is
something — animals without cages."

Grandpa Fred got his jacket out of the closet and put a blue watch-cap on his head. "What did you do with your cap, John?"

John said, "I didn't wear one." He looked at Grandpa Fred's cap. "I think Grandma Jane is making me a red one like yours."

"Sure am." She gave him a hug. "I'll finish it by tomorrow, too, unless a certain grandson makes me bake cookies all evening."

"Do I get to vote?" asked Grandpa Fred.

"About what?" they asked together.

"Whether you make a hat or make cookies."

John shook his head. "Not this time, Grandpa Fred."

But as they went out the door John winked at him. The chances of getting cookies before the hat was finished looked pretty good.